Printed with Sylexiad Serif
Easy-reading font

© 2017 La Grafica Pisana, Italy
ISBN 978-88-97732-42-6
Translated by Livia Del Rosso
Edizioni La Grafica Pisana
Collana Andalù

Pinocchio

by Carlo Collodi

Illustrated by Daria Palotti

Andalù®

Edizioni La Grafica Pisana

One fine day, a piece of wood was delivered to Mr. Cherry-o's shop – a carpenter so-called because of his big red nose, which indeed reminded everyone of a cherry.

Mr. Cherry-o had the intention to shape the log as a table leg, but as soon as he raised his hatchet to let go the first blow he heard a wee little voice:

"Don't hit me!"

The carpenter, shocked, remained with his arm suspended in the air.

"I must have figured out that little voice", he said, and he struck a hard blow upon the piece of wood.

"Ohi! You hurt me!"

Mr. Cherry-o remained frozen, mouth wide open. It was impossible that the log had spoken! He decided to strike another blow, but the little voice piped up again. Mr. Cherry-o had no idea what to do, he was so frightened.

Luckily, in that very moment he was interrupted by his friend Geppetto, who was looking for a piece of wood to carve a puppet. This was the perfect opportunity to get rid of the weird voice that came from the log – a log!

Once at home, Geppetto, wasting no time, started to make his marionette. Talking to himself, he had the idea to name it Pinocchio.

First, he shaped the head, then he focused on the eyes and the mouth. While the man was working, he noticed that the puppet was smiling, laughing, and making fun of him.

As soon as he carved the nose, this started to grow bigger and bigger. Geppetto tried to carve and shape it again but he was too slow and couldn't keep up.

After a while, the carpenter relented, the nose would grow anyway and it didn't seem to bother Pinocchio, since he was laughing very hard.

After the face was shaped, Geppetto carved his neck, shoulders, chest, arms and hands, and as soon as they were ready, Pinocchio quickly ripped off the carpenter's blonde wig.

Bothered by the puppet's pranks, Geppetto tried to finish the missing parts as quickly as possible.

Legs, knees, ankles, and feet – now the marionette was finally ready, and the carpenter stood up to admire his work. He didn't even have time to think that Pinocchio jumped up and ran across the room, dashing out the front door.

Geppetto ran after Pinocchio, shouting to everybody:

"Catch him! Catch him!"

But the bystanders could do nothing but laugh, seeing a puppet running away from an old man.

All the chaos drew the attention of two policemen. One of them managed to catch Pinocchio by the nose and gave him back to the carpenter, who was panting due to the effort of running after him.

Geppetto, exhausted and furious, forcefully tried to lead Pinocchio back home, but the spectators started hissing and shouting at him.

"Poor puppet!"

"Who knows what that evil man is going to do to him?!"

"If you let him go, he will tear it apart!"

"That poor marionette was right to run away from home!"

Hearing these words, the policemen let Pinocchio go and took Geppetto, who started to cry as he was being dragged to prison.

While Geppetto was being forced to go to prison, Pinocchio went home, where he found Jeremiah the Cricket. The strange insect decided to tell the puppet an important truth:

"Shame on all the boys that betray their parents, that don't go to school or learn a job. They all end up in hospital or in jail".

These words bothered Pinocchio, who shouted:

"Shut up Cricket! I don't want to go to school, I prefer having fun, climbing trees and playing whenever I want to!"

The Cricket kept talking, but soon the puppet got so furious that he grabbed a wooden hammer and instantly killed the insect.

Night came and Pinocchio started to feel hungry and sad. He was now all alone and missed Geppetto. The puppet was so cold and tired that he fell asleep in front of the fireplace, but during the night his wooden feet got burnt.

Luckily Geppetto came home the day after, he brought three pears for breakfast and helped Pinocchio repair his burnt feet.

The marionette promised to go to school the next day. The carpenter was so poor that he had to sell his only jacket to buy a spelling book.

The next day, Pinocchio woke up full of good intentions. He was on his way to school when he heard a strange music of flutes and drums. Forgetting about school, he followed the sounds until he reached the Great Puppet Theatre, where, drawn by curiosity, he sold his precious spelling book to buy a ticket.

The marionettes in the theatre immediately recognized him, inviting him to join them on stage. In doing so, they interrupted the performance, making the terrible puppet master very angry. Fire-Eater was his name, he wanted to use Pinocchio to poke the fire he was using to roast a ram for dinner.

Hearing this, the puppet started to cry and told Fire-Eater the story of his poor father.

The puppet master was heavily moved, he saved Pinocchio's life and in addition, he gave him five precious golden coins.

These golden coins were in fact, for poor Geppetto, who,

despite the snow and the cold, sold his only jacket to send Pinocchio to school.

The puppet and the puppet master warmly bid each other farewell and Pinocchio left to return home.

While he was walking, he met a strange couple. One was blind and the other was walking with a limp, and they walked along supporting each other.

They were the Tomcat and the She-Fox, who, after listening to the story of the kind Fire-Eater, smartly convinced the puppet to follow them in their quest to the Miracle Meadow. Here, Pinocchio could bury the five golden coins, and the next day he would be able to collect many more. So they left, and in the evening, tired and exhausted, they reached the Red Crab Inn.

"Let's stop here to eat something", said the She-Fox. "At midnight, after resting for a good couple of hours, we will leave again for the Miracle Meadow."

So they stopped at the Red Crab Inn and quickly sat at the table, ravenously hungry.

The courses were many and varied – meat, fish, cheese, vegetables...

When the Tomcat and the She-Fox were finally full, they decided to take a room to rest until the appointed time.

Pinocchio also decided to have a quick nap before departing again, but he was suddenly woken up in the middle of the night by the innkeeper. The man told him that his friends had left two hours before, and furthermore, they had forgotten to pay for the dinner.

The puppet paid the host with one of his golden coins and dashed outside, determined to reach the Tomcat and She-Fox. However, the night was so dark that it was impossible to see, so Pinocchio was forced to move forward blindly, slowly, and full of fear.

Eventually, Pinocchio saw what seemed to be two hooded black figures in the dark. They were the Tomcat and She-Fox, dressed up as two assassins in order to be unrecognizable.

Pinocchio tried to run away, but he was grabbed from the collar! He was so scared that he put the four golden coins into his mouth. He heard voices shouting:

"You cannot run from us now!"

"Open your mouth, will you?"

The two murderers had two sharp knives, which they didn't hesitate to use to stab the poor puppet in the back. Luckily, the wood Pinocchio was made of was so hard that it broke the blades into pieces.

"Hang him!" one of the two hooded assassins said. The She-Fox was holding the marionette, and the Tomcat was tying his legs, arms, and neck with a rope. They hanged the poor puppet under a big oak and there they stood, waiting for him to spit out the golden coins, but after two hours, the assassins decided to come back the day after because they were tired of waiting.

In the wood where Pinocchio was hung, there lived a pretty maiden with azure hair. She saw the puppet from her window and ordered him to be put to bed, and then called Three Doctors to visit him.

Shortly after, a Crow, an Owl and a Cricket arrived, and argued if the marionette was dead or alive.

Pinocchio woke up after some time, but he was ill with a high temperature, and had to take a bitter medicine. The puppet refused it several times, but when he saw the black rabbits carrying his coffin, he decided to take the medicine even if it was unpleasant.

The Fairy maiden then asked him how he had ended up in the assassins' hands and Pinocchio told her his story. He talked about Geppetto and the Fire-Eater, how he had met the Tomcat and She-Fox and about the golden coins he was going to bury in the Miracle Meadow.

"Where are the golden coins now?", asked the pretty Fairy.

"I lost them", answered Pinocchio.

But as soon as he told the lie, his nose started to grow.

The Fairy asked him for a few more questions, but the puppet replied with more lies, and as a result his nose kept growing longer and longer until it was as big as the room they were in.

Pinocchio, seeing that his nose had gotten so big, started to cry. The Fairy left him like that for some minutes, as she wanted him to regret his lies. She then called some little birds, specifically woodpeckers.

The woodpeckers started to peck at the puppet's nose which was brought to the right size again. The marionette was so happy that he thanked the Fairy, who had helped him when he was ill and also called Geppetto.

Knowing that he would be seeing his father again, Pinocchio jumped out of his bed and decided to meet him halfway to hug him as soon as possible.

He said a quick goodbye to the Fairy and left, taking the path through the woods.

While he was walking, Pinocchio found the Tomcat and She-Fox again.

"Here is our beloved Pinocchio!"

They immediately asked him about his golden coins.

"I still have them in my pocket", answered Pinocchio, "But I spent one to pay for the dinner at the Red Crab Inn."

The two crooks then convinced him to go to the Miracle Meadow, so that he could make Geppetto a wealthy man.

Under the She-Fox lead, they reached a field that didn't look any different from a normal one. Pinocchio dug a small hole in the ground and buried the four remaining coins, then went to the closest town to rest for the day.

But when he went back to the Miracle Meadow the next day, he did not find a golden-coin-tree as he was promised, because during the night the Tomcat and She-Fox dug the coins up and stole them all.

Hungry for the misfortune, Pinocchio stopped in a vineyard to eat some grapes. He was spotted by the owner who, as a punishment, made the puppet be his watchdog, since the previous one, Mold Foot, had died.

The task Pinocchio was given was to guard the chickens at night. From the kennel, in the middle of the night, Pinocchio saw something moving near the henhouse. There were some weasels whispering to each other.

The puppet then started to bark, just like a dog. This woke the farmer up, who was finally able to catch the thieves.

As a reward the man released Pinocchio, who headed back towards home.

He reached the seaside and saw a small boat with Geppetto on board.

He tried to call him, shouting and waving his arms, but the boat was swallowed by the rough waves.

Fearful that his father could drown, Pinocchio jumped into the sea, determined to save the poor man. After some hours, though, tired by the effort to find Geppetto, he let the current bring him back to shore.

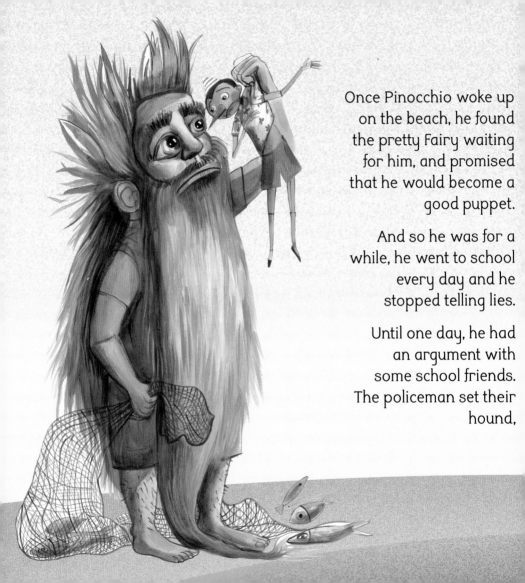

Once Pinocchio woke up
on the beach, he found
the pretty Fairy waiting
for him, and promised
that he would become a
good puppet.

And so he was for a
while, he went to school
every day and he
stopped telling lies.

Until one day, he had
an argument with
some school friends.
The policeman set their
hound,

Goldenwing, after him, but the dog fell into the sea and asked the puppet for help because he couldn't swim.

Pinocchio, kindly, saved him. The marionette, all wet and cold, decided to go into a nearby cave to heat by the fire he saw. But he was caught in the fishing net of a green giant, who was catching some fish to fry in a pan.

Scared, Pinocchio hid between the fish, until he remained the last one and was breaded by the giant, ready to be fried.

When everything seemed to be lost, Goldenwing suddenly appeared and bit the giant fisherman, repaying the puppet for his favour earlier. Pinocchio ran away with the hound and came back to the beloved Fairy.

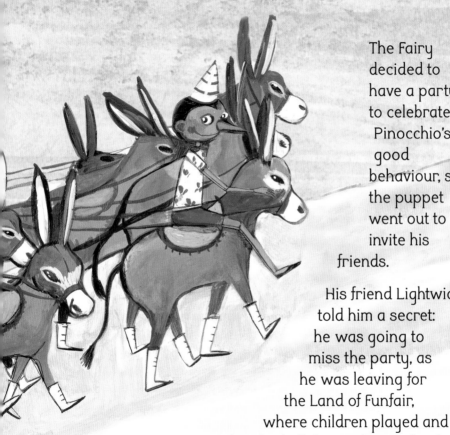

The Fairy decided to have a party to celebrate Pinocchio's good behaviour, so the puppet went out to invite his friends.

His friend Lightwick told him a secret: he was going to miss the party, as he was leaving for the Land of Funfair, where children played and laughed all day with no school or parents. So that when the cart dragged by donkeys came, Pinocchio, who couldn't resist such a temptation, left together with his friend Lightwick.

The Land of Funfair was indeed the dream of every child, the streets were filled with theatres and marionettes, endless games, sweets and happiness.

After five months of limitless fun, one day Pinocchio realised that a pair of long hairy donkey's ears had grown up on his head.

Lightwick had them too. Little by little the two of them were turning into donkeys!

First the ears, then the tail, and then they started to bray, until two donkeys were standing where Pinocchio and Lightwick had been before.

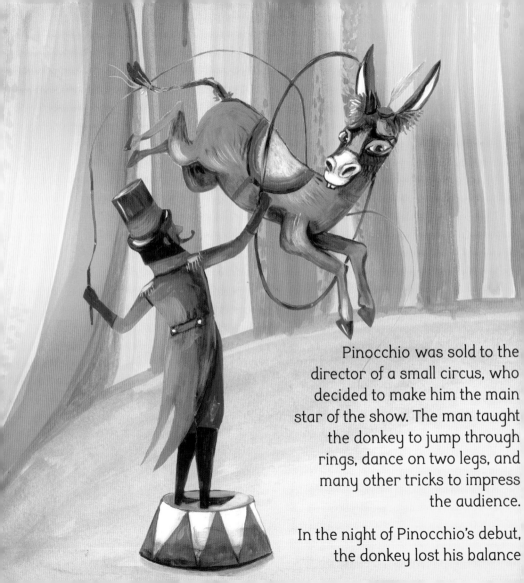

Pinocchio was sold to the director of a small circus, who decided to make him the main star of the show. The man taught the donkey to jump through rings, dance on two legs, and many other tricks to impress the audience.

In the night of Pinocchio's debut, the donkey lost his balance during a jump, injuring one of his legs. The director was so angry that he decided to sell the animal to a friend who needed the skin to make a drum, as it was unable to be part of the performance anymore.

Sold for 20 coins, the donkey was given to the new owner who decided to make the animal drown in order to avoid ruining the skin for the drum. A rope ending in a big rock was tied to Pinocchio's legs, to drag him down to the bottom of the sea.

But as soon as the man threw the donkey into the sea, something magical happened and a wooden puppet appeared, floating on the water.

"Where's the donkey I threw into the sea?", the man exclaimed, his eyes open wide.

"That donkey is me", answered Pinocchio, "Farewell!"

And saying this, the puppet started to swim away. However his happiness didn't last long because after a few metres he was swallowed by a giant whale.

Help! Help! Poor me! Is nobody coming to save me?!"

"Who is supposed to save you?", said a voice from the darkness.

"Who's talking?", asked Pinocchio with a shaky voice.

"I am a poor Tuna-Fish, swallowed by the Whale just like you. Give up, the only thing to do is to wait for the Whale to digest us. I wish you could run away with all my heart".

Pinocchio said goodbye to the Tuna-Fish and went further down the belly of the whale where he glimpsed a feeble light. The puppet then saw a small table with a candle on and a tiny old man, so white-haired and frail that he seemed to be made of snow. Pinocchio was full of joy seeing poor Geppetto again. He dashed to him, laughing, crying, and shouting, he was so excited.

"Are my eyes deceiving me? Is that you for real, my dear Pinocchio?", cried Geppetto, just as moved as the puppet.
"It's me indeed! How long have you been here?"
"Almost a year", answered Geppetto sadly.

The old man then told Pinocchio how his boat sank, together with a large merchant vessel, both swallowed by the Whale. In the vessel there was can food, almost finished now, and paper, ink, wood, and a few candles.

"Father", said Pinocchio, "There's no time to lose! We need to escape from the Whale's mouth!"

Bear in mind that the Whale was very old and suffered from asthma, so it slept with its mouth open.

In fact, Pinocchio and Geppetto reached the mouth without difficulty. Through the opening, they saw a breathtaking sky filled with stars and a calm sea.

"This is the moment to escape, come on papa!", said Pinocchio softly. He didn't want to wake the Whale up.

The two of them walked on tiptoes on Its tongue and overcame three rows of sharp teeth. Then Pinocchio said to Geppetto in a voice as low as possible:

"Climb onto my shoulders and let me take care of the rest".

While Pinocchio was swimming towards the shore, he realized that the old man was shaking. The puppet tried his best to look in a good mood, he pretended the beach was close and the water not so cold. But after a while, both Pinocchio and Geppetto were exhausted and were about to drown. Suddenly something was coming closer and closer...

"I know you, you are Pinocchio! I am the Tuna-Fish, your friend inside the stomach of the Whale! I followed your example and escaped myself".

"Oh Tuna!", said Pinocchio, "Help us please, or we are lost!"

So the two of them climbed on the top of the Tuna-Fish who carried them to the shore, saving the life of the puppet and his father.

Pinocchio and Geppetto said goodbye to the Tuna-Fish, then they slowly went home.

From then on, the puppet started to work from morning to evening to help Geppetto.

One day, the puppet heard that the Fairy was seriously ill. He immediately decided to go and visit her and give her all his savings, so that she could be treated by the best doctors.

The Fairy was not actually ill at all. She was in fact in perfect health, and just wanted to test the puppet's kindness.

Having overcome this final test, the Fairy gave Pinocchio many golden coins and finally turned him into a real boy.

And what about the marionette?

It was left sitting on a chair with its arms dangling, to remind Pinocchio how funny he once looked.

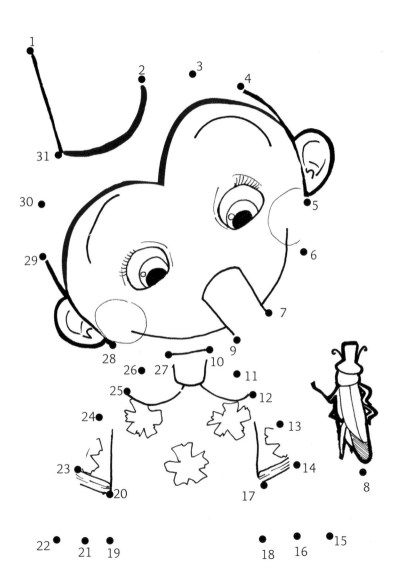